The Red Umbrella

Jessica Baverstock

Creative Ark

The Red Umbrella

This edition first published in 2017

Copyright © 2014 by Jessica Baverstock
Published by Creative Ark
Cover design © Jessica Baverstock
Cover art © cranach/iStock

All rights are reserved. This book or any portion thereof may not be reproduced or used in any manner whatsoever without the express written permission of the publisher except for the use of brief quotations in a book review.

This is a work of fiction. Names, characters, businesses, places, events and incidents are either the products of the author's imagination or used in a fictitious manner. Any resemblance to actual persons, living or dead, or actual events is purely coincidental.
(Except for the bit about the pigeon. That actually happened, but the location of the boucherie has been changed to protect the identity of the bird.)

I would like to say that no animals were harmed in the making of this book, but actually one pigeon was slightly dazed and lost some tail feathers while this book was being researched. It was purely accidental, I swear.

ISBN: 1534625143
ISBN-13: 978-1534625143

THE RED UMBRELLA

PAULIE DASHED DOWN the hallway to the coat rack and cupboard by the door.

Scarf.

Coat.

Shoes.

Or boots?

Shoes were more comfortable, but boots were warmer.

Nannette would have told her – and have predicted the weather just by glancing out the window – but for this week Paulie was on her own.

Shoes.

No, boots.

Paulie stopped herself and took a deep breath.

Stop rushing. She could do this. For crying out loud, she wasn't a little girl any more. Just because her roommate had gone away for a few days didn't mean her life was going to fall apart. Goodness, she was now a university student, beginning her life of world travels. She didn't need someone holding her hand.

1

The country outside her front door was home – at least for the next year – and she was going to conquer it.

Boots.

She straightened. Her long brown hair was caught in her scarf, but that was easily fixed with a flick of her hand.

Okay. She was set.

She picked up her bag, slung it over her shoulder, then reached for her umbrella.

She smiled. Her red umbrella always made her smile.

She picked it up and ran her finger along the curved plastic handle. *Where would I be without you?*

Last-minute check: keys, ID, pack of tissues, phone, map, money, phrasebook, class textbook, notepad, pen, spare pen. And umbrella, of course.

She took one more deep breath and then let herself out of the apartment.

In the hallway she pushed the button for the lift, then pushed it again with an extra, urgent jiggle. The hum of the machinery grew louder and had almost reached her floor when the door to apartment 16 opened.

Paulie sighed. She considered taking the stairs, but the neighbour had already spotted her.

"*Bonjour*," said the short man with a smile and nod.

"*Bonjour*," Paulie nodded in return. To take the stairs now would be impolite.

It's not that she had anything against the little man. It was the lift she disliked.

The door opened, revealing a space not much bigger than a coffin. French lifts were made for one person – even if the notice insisted six could fit. To share such a space with another was an extremely intimate experience when compared to the commodious lifts back home in Melbourne.

The man gestured for her to enter and then followed her in.

She held the umbrella handle to her chest, its furled material shielding her. As the lift lurched and began its descent, she turned her attention to the ceiling.

The man muttered something in French.

Paulie glanced at him and noticed his enquiring gaze. "*Pardon?*" she said. She felt silly saying such words in French. To her ear she just seemed to be speaking English with a fake accent, which felt disrespectful. And yet, honestly, this was the way people spoke.

"*Comment ça va?*" the man said.

"Oh." Her mind whirred for a split-second before she responded, "*Très bien*," the aspirated first syllable tickling the back of her throat.

The man smiled and spoke again, this time his words too fast to decipher.

Paulie froze, considering her options. She could smile and nod, but what if he were telling her of some ailment? "*Oui*" was probably a safe bet – as people usually liked to be agreed with – unless this was one of those occasions when "*Non*" was the proper response. Or she could try "*Bon*," but she always felt like she'd just stepped out of a Poirot episode when she said that. Then there was "*D'accord*," which also implied agreement, but was this one of those times when agreement was needed?

In the end she simply giggled and shrugged her shoulders.

The man nodded, friendly but resigned, and turned his own attention to the ceiling.

The lift jerked to a stop. Its doors opened and Paulie and the man both exited. With a mutual, "*Au revoir*," they parted ways.

Paulie stepped into the outdoors to find a gentle rain pattering down.

She opened her umbrella, its long wire arms reaching out and protecting her. Each droplet made a soft tap as it hit the waterproof fabric – detoured to the ground by the red canopy, leaving her dry.

As she made her way to the Metro, she noted the people she passed. A few sheltered from the drizzle under the awning of the general store and took the opportunity to engage each other in conversation. Others pulled the collars of their coats up around their ears, dug their hands into their pockets and kept walking. Some had remembered to carry umbrellas, blue or black or green, but she held the only red one on the whole street.

Paulie loved the rain. Water showed a place off to its best. It was nature's way of wiping down doors, windows, walls and polishing leaves and flowers – leaving behind perfect, clear, sparkling droplets that caught the sunlight like diamonds.

Her boots made a wonderful splashing sound as she marched towards the station, the cobblestone street beneath her feet shining like it had just been lacquered.

As she descended the stairs to the Metro, she carefully closed her umbrella, tucking each fold of fabric into position. She ran her finger over the velcro strap's frayed edges, recalling how many times she had caught herself fiddling with it when she was nervous. Had she fiddled with it in the lift that morning? She didn't think so.

She hooked the umbrella handle over her arm, freeing her hands to fish her travel card out of her pocket. She swiped the card and stepped through the gates, then descended another set of stairs on to the platform. The clock suggested she could make it to class on time, but it would require a brisk walk after a punctual train.

The quiet of the station platform was broken by the whipping sound relayed along the rails, heralding the train. Paulie stepped forward in preparation. The doors don't open themselves, she reminded herself as the train rumbled into view. It was those simple little things that still caught her out after three weeks of trial and error, embarrassing as well as confusing.

The train eased to a stop. Paulie grabbed hold of the door handle, moving it in an arc as Nannette had shown her, and was relieved when the doors flew open. The mechanism still made no sense, but at least she could operate it.

She stepped on board and chose a seat near a middle-aged woman reading a paperback. As the train began moving again, Paulie surreptitiously inspected the occupants of the carriage.

A group of primary school-aged children were seated across from her, deep in conversation. She had noted young French children seemed more serious and self-assured than Australian or English children, although she had not yet befriended one to test her assumption. She considered whether now was a good time to start a conversation with one of them, but nerves got the better of her. After all, they were in a group. Perhaps it would be easier to try making friends with just one or two children.

Further along the carriage sat a man with white

hair and a checkered scarf. He seemed to be surveying the other passengers with a similar curiosity. Paulie averted her eyes as his gaze passed her. Although she loved watching people, she hated the awkwardness of actually catching another person's eye. For a few moments she inspected the buttons of her coat in the hope she had not drawn his attention.

When she looked up again and surveyed the opposite side of the carriage, she noted a young couple, the woman leaning her head into the shoulder of the young man as he drew her closer to him. They talked softly to each other and smiled – at ease in each other's company and yet buzzing with excitement at being together. She couldn't help wondering about the effect of French whispers. But there would be plenty of time for that once she'd mastered the language.

The language! She came to her senses with a start. What was the next station? Before she had simply waited for Nannette to stand up and then followed suit, but today she had to be self-reliant. She caught the end of the announcement as the train began slowing, but couldn't recognise it. Her mind seemed even more sluggish today than normal. She leaned forward and looked out the window as the train pulled into the station.

The familiar signs of Cluny La Sorbonne came into view but she didn't trust her judgement until the train stopped and she could yank the door open to let herself out. Glancing up she saw the colourful mosaics across the ceiling. Yes, this was her stop. She sighed. Goodness knows where she could have ended up if she hadn't come to her senses.

Trotting up the stairs she chided herself on how

much she'd relied on Nannette. She could not be a world traveller if she wasn't able to look after herself.

The people in front of her opened their umbrellas as they reached the top of the stairs. Paulie reached for her umbrella.

But it wasn't there.

She faltered, her legs halting in mid-stride. It should be hanging on her arm. Had it fallen?

She dashed back down the stairs, looking along each step and even at the umbrellas held by those passing her. Perhaps someone had picked it up.

Finding nothing she swiped her travel card again and returned to the station platform. Perhaps, just perhaps it was somewhere there?

But already there was the sinking feeling of realisation. The last time she had seen the umbrella was when she sat down on the train. She had no recollection of picking it up as she left.

A lump formed in her throat. Was it really gone?

The rumble of the next train gave her hope. Could she get on this train and follow it? At the final station, maybe she could dash across to the other side of the platform and it would be waiting for her. Or maybe there would be a station master to explain her plight to.

Somehow.

In French.

Or with hand signals.

The train doors opened as people got off and she hovered in the doorway, deliberating.

It was her red umbrella. Her friend. She could not just abandon it. There had to be a way to find it.

Together, she and her umbrella had been through thick and thin for over ten years. They'd travelled to New Zealand when she was twelve and to Los

Angeles when she was sixteen. Now they'd made it to Europe and it was just the beginning of a lifetime of adventures. It couldn't be over now, so soon.

The doors closed, bringing her back to her senses.

It was no use. The umbrella was gone.

She knew it, but it wasn't yet real.

With a deep breath she centred herself. There would be time to come to terms with what happened. Right now she was an adult on her way to university, running late for class. She could get through the day without an umbrella.

In a daze, she forced herself back towards the stairs.

***

By the time she returned to street level, the drizzle had finally stopped. The faint rays of the sun were encroaching on the clouds, promising a reprieve from the gloom that started the day.

Paulie wandered along the alleys trying to retrace the route Nannette had taken her each morning. Her mind was stunned, still processing the split-second mistake that she would no doubt berate herself over for years to come. She barely took in her surroundings as her feet progressed along the pavement, following muscle memory until she came to the gates of the university.

The gates were closed.

She stared at the building. She was in the right place.

But the gates were closed.

No other students were milling around, waiting to be admitted.

Just her.

And then she realised her mistake.

There was no class today.

It was Saturday.

Her shoulders slumped. There had been no need to panic this morning. No need to rush breakfast, get dressed, leave home – no need to take the Metro and no need to hop off in such a hurry. No need to leave a precious possession behind.

She sat down on the edge of a stone wall and sighed. The sunshine broke through the clouds, shining on the wet ground.

There was nothing she could do about it now. What was done was done – a principle that applied to both the lost umbrella and her needless commute. The real question worth considering now was: What was she going to do with her morning?

The first thing that sprang to her mind was to go straight home. She could make herself a hot cup of tea, open a box of chocolates and mope in front of the television.

It was tempting.

But, she quickly reminded herself, she hadn't come halfway around the world just to sit at home feeling sorry for herself.

She would, instead, go shopping.

Not for clothes, although Paulie would have dearly loved to buy herself a beret or a new scarf. Or was that too French? Too clichéd? It was still so hard to know what was naturally French and what was simply her perception of French from childhood movies.

No, the first order of the day was buying food. If she was not going to have lunch at the university today she would cook some comfort food at home.

She hopped up off the wall and began wandering

down the narrow streets, flanked on either side by buildings that had witnessed centuries of history – seen everything from the horse and cart to the Mini Cooper. The realisation of how aged were the walls she passed humbled her every time she thought about it.

In Australia a building was considered old if it had reached a century, yet those buildings were crude when compared to the magnificence of these structures. Some, as ordinary as simple lodgings installed in centuries past, spoke of an artistry that went into their construction and maintenance that made walking through the plainest of alleys journeys of discovery.

One building in particular caught her eye – its intricately carved wooden door, the multi-coloured brickwork of browns, greens, and blues, ornate, arched window frames supported by Roman-style columns. She had never seen such detail in a building back home, yet by Paris standards it was merely a simple back-street residential structure.

She took a deep breath, attempting to absorb everything around her, but it was impossible to take it all in. How would she even hope to fathom the world if the simplest of buildings overwhelmed her?

She walked on, contemplating lunch. A taste of home was in order. Something soothing and warming. The taste of shepherd's pie danced in her memory – her mother's version, with lamb mince, kidney beans, tomato paste, and smooth, creamy mashed potato topped with melted cheddar.

It was not often that the excitement of her new surroundings yielded to homesickness, but this was one of those times. The only cure was to cook something from home.

But, she reminded herself, she had not seen lamb mince in any of the *supermarchés*.

There was nothing for it. She would have to find a butcher.

***

Pleased with the return of her adventurous spirit, even without her red umbrella for company, she delved into her phrasebook and found the term for 'butcher's shop.' It was then a relatively easy thing to wave down a local – a well-dressed young woman with a pleasant smile and a small black poodle on a leash – and say, "*Boucherie?*" with an enquiring wiggle of the eyebrows.

"Ah, a butcher's shop." The woman spoke beautiful English and provided directions.

And so, a short while later, she found herself staring across a road at the local *boucherie*. It looked very similar to a butcher's back home, with a shop window full of assorted preserved meats and an L-shaped counter inside the store housing a wide selection of chicken and red meat.

As she crossed the road, her phrasebook still in hand and the word for 'lamb' underlined in case she needed to refer to it again, her stomach began to churn. What if they did not understand her? What if they asked her a question she couldn't make out?

Stop your worrying, she told herself. *After all, what's the worst that can happen?*

A woman was already inside the shop, chatting with the butcher over the counter while her son squatted outside watching the pigeons. He seemed particularly taken with a bird limping from the loss of a foot. As Paulie approached, the woman called the boy, waving for him to come inside and leave the birds alone. He obeyed, pouting as he shot a final look at them over his shoulder.

Paulie paused outside the shop, closing her eyes for a moment and centring herself.

The process was simple. Enter the shop, ask for lamb, pay and leave.

She stepped inside, head held high, ready to make eye contact with the butcher.

The butcher glanced at her and gave the universal nod indicating he would be with her in a moment.

Meanwhile the little boy started chatting to his mother. He tugged on his mother's sleeve, attempting to interrupt her discussion with the butcher, becoming more and more urgent, pointing at Paulie.

The boy's attention unnerved Paulie. Was there something wrong with the way she was dressed? No doubt the phrase book she clutched in her hand gave her away as a foreigner. She shoved the book into her bag, but still the boy pointed at her.

She stepped backwards, hoping she could blend into the background until the woman and child had left.

And then it happened.

From behind Paulie there erupted a frantic fluttering. She turned in time to see a poor little pigeon take flight inside the shop. Somehow she had herded it in as she entered.

She ducked to make room for it, but the bird had already formed an exit strategy. It flew across the shop heading for the small patch of visible blue sky, only realising its mistake when it slammed into the shop window. It slid down the glass and landed among the hams. From there it began hobbling across the preserved meats in a vain attempt at gaining freedom. With horror Paulie recognised it as the one-footed bird she had seen earlier.

The mother was now clutching her son to her, watching the proceedings wide-eyed. Paulie felt some responsibility for the bird now busy contaminating the butcher's wares, but there was nothing she could do. In her agitation, she caught herself fiddling with a loose edge of her coat lining.

The butcher, a large man with a hefty chest and round, strong hands, calmly grabbed the pigeon by the tail and lifted it out of the window display. The bird beat its wings as the butcher walked towards the rear of his shop.

For a dreadful moment Paulie thought he was going to continue walking straight through the doorway into the back room and slaughter the poor thing then and there. It was meat, after all, and there were plenty of pigeons about. She glanced at a bird carcass displayed in the poultry section and wondered at its origin.

But the butcher turned, following the L shape of his counter until he reached the opening next to the till. He stepped through the gap, towards Paulie. Without thinking she grabbed for her umbrella to protect herself, but it was not there.

He continued past her, heading outside the shop. With a flick of his wrist he launched the bird into the sky. The pigeon took to flight and did not look back, leaving only a spattering of tail feathers behind him.

The little boy darted outside the shop and grabbed at the descending feathers. Holding one up to the sky with the air of a conquering hero, he declared, "*Plumage magique!*"

Meanwhile the butcher returned to his spot behind the counter and continued wrapping the lady's order in paper, seemingly unperturbed by the contaminants Paulie was sure had just been spread across his meat display in the window.

With a shudder, Paulie turned and walked out of the shop, passing the boy who was lovingly stroking his newly acquired magic feather. She didn't know whether her urge to leave was because of a valid concern for her health, or simply the overwhelming embarrassment at the incident she'd just caused.

Whichever it was, she made a mental note never again to use the phrase, 'What's the worst that could happen?' Clearly she had underestimated the disasters possible in a foreign land.

She looked down at the inside of her coat where she had caught herself fiddling with the lining. The edge of it had come loose from the stitching and was beginning to fray.

With a stamp of her foot she decided. She needed to buy herself a new umbrella.

***

Paulie attacked umbrella shopping with gusto. She dutifully entered any shop that looked like it would sell umbrellas – from clothing shops to souvenir shops and even a shop full of Venetian masks – saying "*Bonjour*" each time she entered and "*Au revoir*" when she exited.

She enjoyed the custom of acknowledging people as she shopped. While she preferred browsing the shops without assistance, avoiding the stress of having to explain her quest in French each time, she did appreciate the friendly atmosphere that was immediately created by the simple, happy greeting. Truth be told, she also liked saying the words because they rolled off her tongue so easily. Through everyday use they had worked their way into her natural vocabulary, no longer requiring thought or contortions of the mouth – they simply came when she wanted them. If only all French words were that obedient.

There were plenty of umbrellas to choose from. There were tall ones, that would scrape along the ground when the long curved handles hung from her arm. There were long ones with straight handles that couldn't nestle in the crook of her arm. There were small ones that collapsed into a tight bundle that would fit in a bag, but Paulie disliked the idea of shoving a wet umbrella in her bag even if it did come with its own little cover. There were deep umbrellas that seemed to envelop her, covering down to her shoulders when open and providing a clear plastic panel through which to navigate the streets, making her feel like she was suffocating in a plastic bubble. There were elegant lace umbrellas, completely impractical for everyday use. There were umbrellas built for two, reaching out twice as wide as a normal umbrella but not at all suitable for a single girl in the narrow alleys of Paris.

The available colours ranged from simple blacks and blues to checks and even tartans. One umbrella had alternating panels of vanilla white and chocolate brown. It appealed to her, except for the fact that it did not have a long, uniform brim but fabric that came to a point at the end of each metal rib. Paulie felt it looked antagonistic and dangerous, and so placed it back on the rack. There were burgundy umbrellas, orange umbrellas, and deep plum umbrellas. But she could not find a red umbrella.

Most plentiful of all were umbrellas with the Eiffel Tower printed on them – displaying a colour or sepia photograph, an abstract painting, a pink shadow on a black background, or a drawing on a fiery red sky that looked like doomsday. Other umbrellas displayed paintings from the local museums or photographs of typical Parisian streets.

But none felt quite right.

By the end of the morning, Paulie believed she had looked at over one hundred umbrellas – and not one of them was suitable to replace what she had lost.

***

She stepped out of the last shop into another sudden downpour.

The rain spat on her head and face as she walked with her shoulders hunched and her collar up around her ears. The water worked its way through her hair and eventually penetrated to her scalp. She squinted to keep the fine drops from her eyes, and so they congregated on her eyelashes instead.

A young couple walked towards her, their arms wrapped around each other as they huddled under a single umbrella. The girl stopped and reached out to tap Paulie on the arm. She offered Paulie a spare umbrella from her bag, but Paulie simply shook her head. The couple shrugged and kept walking.

Paulie knew she was being petulant. After all, an umbrella was an umbrella. It kept one dry in the rain, and that's all that could be asked of it.

But her red umbrella had meant more than that.

It had been given to her on her first day of school. A gift from her grandmother. When she had come into the kitchen for breakfast that morning it was lying on the table, wrapped in brown paper, waiting for her.

The small card attached to it said, "Red is the colour of bravery. With your umbrella in hand, there is nothing you cannot face. Grandma."

It was true.

With her umbrella in hand, she faced many things.

Like the first day of school, with new routines and strange expectations. Stephanie, her best-friend-to-be, asked her why she brought an umbrella to school on a sunny day – a simple question initiating a lifelong friendship.

Then there was her grandmother's funeral. A dark, rainy day with many sad faces and only one red umbrella.

A few years later, she and her umbrella took their first trip on a plane, flying high above the ocean until they reached New Zealand – a whole new country to explore and with it the realisation of how many more fascinating places they had yet to see.

Her umbrella was with her the day she apologised to her mother after their first big argument. She had stood alone under her umbrella for half an hour in the pouring rain, venting her frustrations to the soggy ground before finally finding the words and courage to return to the house and say she was sorry.

And then there was the trip with her dad to Los Angeles. She twisted and fiddled with the velcro strap of her umbrella as they waited to board the plane, wondering what she and her dad would talk about on the long flight together. Two days in Disneyland finally revealed the topics they had in common, and the umbrella was packed in her check-in luggage on the way back.

Then came the day she said goodbye to her parents before stepping aboard the first flight she'd taken without them – just her and her red umbrella, setting off on her adult adventures, leaving behind everything she knew, her parents, her best friend, her bedroom, her favourite foods. But with her umbrella in hand, that one precious object from home, she was ready to embrace her new life of travel.

Now, without it, she wasn't so sure she wanted a life of travel.

She felt she had somehow betrayed her umbrella, after all those years and all those travels to have jumped up and left it on a train.

Her wanderings brought her back to the Cluny La Sorbonne metro station. With a sigh she decided to go home, dry herself off and make grilled tomato and cheese sandwiches for lunch. It wasn't shepherd's pie, but it would be warm and it would taste like home. Perhaps that's where she belonged.

***

She pulled the travel card out of her pocket and swiped it. It was only after she'd passed through the gate she noticed she hadn't missed the feeling of her umbrella in the crook of her arm.

Had she already moved on from her loss? So fast?

As she descended the stairs onto the station platform, she noticed a red umbrella. It rested next to someone sitting on a bench.

A coincidence she thought at first, someone else with a similar umbrella, but as she came closer she noticed the frayed strap and the familiar curved handle, worn from many years of love.

Holding the handle was a man with white hair and a checkered scarf. As their eyes met, he smiled at her and she recognised him from the train.

"This is yours, is it not?" he said, holding the umbrella out to her. He spoke with a soft accent that she could not place. It was not French, but she lacked the experience to pinpoint it. "Paulie?" he added.

"Yes," she said. "How did you know my name and that I am not French?"

"Your name and address are written on the inside of your umbrella."

"*Merci*," she stuttered. She took the umbrella in her hands, feeling a calmness come over her as the waterproof fabric touched her skin. "I cannot thank you enough. But how did you know where to find me?"

"I saw you leave it on the train this morning. So I picked it up, got off at the next station and came back here. I thought perhaps you would return to look for it."

Her eyes widened. "But that was hours ago! Have you been sitting here all that time?"

The man shrugged. "I had nothing special to do today. It gave me an opportunity to find out why there are names on the ceiling here." He pointed at the signatures formed by the mosaic tiles. "I have often wondered about them, so I decided I could hit two birds with the same stone."

Paulie stared at the ceiling. She hadn't properly looked at the designs before, always too busy following Nannette out of the carriage and chatting away to her as they climbed the stairs. "How did you find out about them?"

"I asked someone," he said. "Many people have sat beside me to wait for their trains. Each had many interesting things to say. An art student told me they are signatures of poets, writers, philosophers, artists, scientists, kings and statesmen from this area. Over there is Robespierre, and that one is Richelieu." He pointed the signatures out to her.

She grew dizzy staring at the names, scrawled by people long dead and now turned into works of art.

"It makes one feel quite small, does it not?" he said.

She nodded. "It seems so strange to think of men like that having such ordinary signatures."

He laughed; a soft, warm sound. "We are all of us ordinary people. Even, or perhaps especially, those who do extraordinary things."

Paulie turned her gaze to him. His words made no sense and yet perfect sense at the same time.

The thrum of the train echoed along the tunnel and into the wide station.

"Would you like to come to my home for lunch?" the man said. "My wife would be very happy to meet you."

Paulie faltered for a moment, the childhood adages regarding not trusting strangers rose to mind, but she pushed them aside. She was an adult now, and with her red umbrella back in tow she was prepared for anything.

***

"My name is Hans," he said, as they settled into their seats on the train. "Hans Tilkens."

"Where are you from?" said Paulie. She kept her umbrella held tightly between her knees. She would not forget it this time.

He smiled as he considered her question. "I have been so many places now, I do not know how to answer you. England, Finland, South Africa, Indonesia. My, there have been too many countries to count. I even spent a year in Chile, just to see what it was like. I am only reminded of my nationality by my passport. I suppose I should say I am Dutch."

"How long have you been travelling?" She leaned forward, eager to hear his words.

"Since I was a young man with enough money in my pocket to pay for a ticket. I am a nomad. I cannot stay too long in one place."

"I am the same! I want to be a nomad," she said. "I think it is a wonderful way to live."

"Well," he said, "it has its ups and downs."

Paulie had to nod at this.

He continued, "Some days it is full of adventure and other days it is just difficult, confusing, and maybe even filled with sadness."

"That sounds like my day," she said.

He raised an enquiring eyebrow. It was all the invitation Paulie needed to pour out the woes she'd experienced, from her lost umbrella and needless commute to her fruitless attempts at shopping. She told him of how much her red umbrella meant to her and how grateful she was to have it back. His patient, understanding nods relaxed her until she even found herself relating the dreadful pigeon incident.

In the retelling, her embarrassment turned to

laugher. By the time she and Mr Hans Tilkens exited the train – with the umbrella firmly in Paulie's hand – they could not contain their giggles.

"I was mortified," she said as they climbed the stairs together.

"Why?" he asked.

"Wouldn't you have been?"

He remained quiet for a moment as they passed through the metro gates and up another flight of stairs. When they reached street level he spoke.

"May I offer you some advice, from one nomad to another?"

"Please," said Paulie.

"This umbrella of yours," he said, walking on slowly, "You should not use it."

Paulie frowned. The rain clouds had once again parted to allow the sunshine through, so she had no intention of opening her umbrella. "I don't understand," she said.

"When people travel for a short time, they usually want to be safe. They want to go somewhere different, but just a little bit different, you know?"

Paulie nodded.

"But," he continued, tucking the end of his scarf into his coat, "a nomad is not this way. They go somewhere different to embrace the difference, to learn from it. Is this how you want your life to be?"

"Yes," she said, almost skipping with excitement. "I want to see new places. Meet people. Experience things."

"But you cannot do that with your umbrella."

"But you don't understand," she said. "It's exactly what I do with my umbrella. I've always done new things with it. Red is the colour of bravery."

He stopped walking and smiled kindly at her. "You use it to shield yourself from life. It is like the comfort blanket of a small child."

Paulie caught herself raising the umbrella to her chest as he spoke, retreating from his words.

"The story of Paulie and her red umbrella is a lovely one, but it is like a children's book. Real life, especially the life of a nomad, is not this way. You cannot hold back from it, or hide from it. You must jump into it and enjoy it all – the good and the bad, the fun and the difficulties. To shield yourself from what frightens you is to miss out on all the extraordinary things. Today you experienced something wonderful at the *boucherie*."

"Wonderful?" said Paulie, feeling heat rising in her cheeks.

"Yes. You have started making new stories – stories without your umbrella. Stories of travel, and adventure, and experiences you would never have dreamed of back in your home town. It is a … what is the term? Rite of passage?"

Paulie nodded.

He smiled and continued, "A rite of passage as a nomad. These things will happen as we go to new places, speak new languages and meet new people. There is no need to be ashamed. Embrace it! That is what you have come here for."

His words gradually made their mark, softening the strain in her neck and shoulders and relaxing her arms. It would take a little while to fully understand what he had said to her, she knew, but she had grasped the gist of it.

She had come all this way to sample an exciting new life, and yet she had shied away from it in so many ways. Her fears of saying something wrong or doing something embarrassing were holding her back from the very things she'd come here to experience.

"I can see your mind is working. Let's eat while you are thinking," he said, pointing to a nearby building.

***

Hans's wife, Anke, did not seem at all surprised to find Hans had brought a new friend home for lunch. She was a tubby woman with a red glow about her face, who insisted on kissing Paulie on both cheeks in greeting.

"Hans is always meeting someone on the train, or in a park and bringing them back here," she said, as she dished out soup into three bowls. "So I always make extra."

"You don't mind him bringing strangers home with him?" said Paulie. Had this been Paulie's home, she would not have been so calm.

Anke smiled. "Of course not. He has many interesting conversations in his day, then he comes home and tells me about them. If he brings someone with him, then I can have an interesting conversation too." She winked at Paulie.

"Oh," said Paulie. "The pressure is on me then to make interesting conversation."

"No, no," said Hans, sitting himself down at the table and gesturing for Paulie to do the same. "There is no need for pressure. Being yourself is interesting."

But as it turned out, Paulie did very little talking except to ask Hans and Anke questions about their travels. The two of them easily slipped into relating their favourite stories.

Hans fondly recalled being cheated by a taxi driver in Shanghai. "It cost me one hundred yuan to learn that lesson, but it was money well spent," he said. "You must not view the loss of money as being swindled. It is the fee for your tuition in life."

Anke then explained how she fell into the Trevi Fountain in Rome. "Can you imagine?" she said, her hands against her cheeks. "There I was completely wet, down to my underwear, and my dress turned see-through."

Hans laughed heartily at this, while Paulie asked, "What did you do?"

"Well, it was a warm day," Anke said with a shrug. "I soon dried out."

Then they moved on to their favourite language *faux pas*.

"Anke and I were invited to a Colombian couple's sixtieth wedding anniversary. During the evening the wife drank too much and took a small tumble. She was unhurt, but I went to inform her husband. I tried to be discreet about it, telling him his wife 'was a little embarrassed,' but I used the Spanish word '*embarazada*.' Without realising it, I had told him his eighty-year-old wife was pregnant! You should have seen the expression on his face."

Now it was Anke's turn to laugh heartily, and Paulie couldn't help but join in.

"This is the way to learn language," said Hans with a grin. "Just give it a go. Mistakes are how you learn."

Before Paulie knew it, the afternoon was nearing its end and she felt it was time to leave.

"Feel free to come around any time," Anke said to

Paulie as she kissed her cheek. "We love to have visitors."

"Have I been interesting enough to have back again?" Paulie asked, looking at Anke and Hans with a twinkle in her eye.

"Of course," said Hans. "Next time you will have to tell us some of your own stories."

"But I don't have any," said Paulie, wide-eyed.

"Well go make some," said Hans.

As she headed towards the door, Paulie saw her red umbrella leaning up against the wall. She put on her coat and wrapped her scarf around her neck, then she pulled on her boots.

"Goodbye," she said to her hosts, as Anke opened the door for her.

"Wait," said Hans. "You have forgotten something."

Paulie glanced back at the umbrella. "I probably won't need it for a while," she said, stepping through the doorway. "Could you look after it for me?"

Hans smiled and nodded.

With a final wave she headed off in the direction of the Metro.

As the drizzle pattered down on her, she turned her face upward and grinned into the rain.

ABOUT THE AUTHOR

Jessica Baverstock lives in Australia with her husband and small book collection. When she's not busy working on her next story or globetrotting across oceans, she likes to curl up with a good movie. You can find a complete list of her books on her website www.jessicabaverstock.com.

If you would like to be kept up to date with Jessica's latest releases and other news, join the newsletter. Go to www.jessicabaverstock.com/newsletter to sign up.

OTHER TITLES BY JESSICA BAVERSTOCK

Short Stories
Baverstock's Allsorts Volume 1
Buried Jewels
The Letterbox
Birdsitting

Novellas
The Clipper Home

Novels
City of Mist
Neville and the Arabian Luncheon

See all available titles at www.jessicabaverstock.com

Printed in Great Britain
by Amazon